Falling for the

Rescue

A Forced Proximity, Search and Rescue Romance Packed with Heat, Heart, and High Stakes

Hana York

Pink Pop Publishing

Falling for the Rescue

(Hearts on Duty Book 5)

Copyright © 2025 by Hana York

www.HanaYork.com

Contents

Chapter One

♥

RYAN

Frigid rain pierced my skin, soaking through my jacket until I was chilled to the bone. One moment, I'd been standing on firm ground, the next—nothing. The earth had crumbled beneath me as a cascade of mud ripped my legs out from under me, dragging me down to the bottom of this godforsaken ravine.

I drew in a sharp breath, my left ankle screaming in protest. Not broken—I'd tested that much—but walking was out of the question. Even worse, my pack had vanished in the chaos.

Grinding my teeth against the frustration bubbling under my skin, I raised my radio. "This is Anderson. I'm stuck in a ravine near marker six. My ankle's injured. I need backup."

Static crackled before the reply came. "Copy that, Anderson. Hold tight. All of our people are tied up, but we have a specialist who is in town for training. I will dispatch them with K9 support to your location."

I exhaled sharply, dragging a hand down my rain-soaked face. "ETA?"

A pause. Then, "As soon as possible. Weather's slowing everything down."

Of course it was.

I shoved my radio back into my vest and leaned against the cold rock face. The downpour was relentless, sheets of rain making everything slick, the ground unstable. I hated waiting. Hated this even more. I wasn't the guy who needed rescuing—I was the one doing the rescuing.

Time crawled by; the only sounds were the storm and the occasional crackle of my radio. Then—something else. Faint but distinct.

Barking.

My head snapped up. I squinted against the rain, scanning the jagged rim of the ravine. A moment later, a voice cut through the storm—sharp, no-nonsense.

"Anderson, you down there?"

"Yeah!" I called back, my pulse kicking up. "About time! You the specialist?"

"Something like that," the voice returned. "Stay put. I'm lowering a harness."

A rope came down with a harness attached. I adjusted my weight, easing the harness over my shoulders and under my legs, wincing as the shift jostled my ankle.

"You good?" The voice came again, firm but focused.

"Yeah, let's do this."

The line went taut, jerking me up inch by painstaking inch. The harness dug into my legs, the rain-slick rope creaking under the weight.

As I neared the top, I expected a strong, calloused hand attached to some burly guy to be there.

Instead, I saw a lithe figure standing back from the edge near a makeshift pulley system, her stance steady despite the mud and rain. Definitely not what I'd expected.

Trough the dim light I caught a glimpse of the setup secured to a sturdy tree just beyond the ravine's edge. Efficient. Clean. Smart. And the woman handling it? Just as steady and sure as the rigging itself, her gloved hands working with practiced precision to pull me up.

The harness gave one last tug, and suddenly, I was over the edge, sprawled on the slick, uneven ground.

It was then I noticed the powerful Chinook dog beside her, muscles taut, standing at attention like he'd been part of the operation the whole time.

Rain slicked off her jacket as she closed the distance between us, her short brown hair plastered to her forehead.

I huffed out a breath, still trying to catch up. "Hell of a setup you've got."

She gave a slight nod, all business. "Gets the job done." Then her gaze flicked up to mine, steady and unwavering.

I exhaled, dragging a hand through my damp hair. "Not gonna lie," I muttered. "Was expecting someone... bigger."

Her lips twitched, but she didn't pause as she crouched next to me, already testing my ankle for damage. "And yet, here you are. Out of the ravine, rescued. Sam Monroe, Search and Rescue from Granite Falls." She jerked her chin toward the dog. "That's Chance."

I let out a breath. "Ryan Anderson. Search and Rescue, Anchor Bay—usually on the other end of these things."

Her lips twitched, just barely. "Guess it's your turn to be rescued."

I huffed. "Not my favorite position."

She crouched beside me, running a quick, practiced eye over me. "Right now, I'm worried about you—can you walk?"

I shifted, testing my ankle, and immediately clenched my jaw against the sharp stab of pain. "Not a chance. Ankle's toast."

She sized me up with a calculating look. "Let me guess—six-four, around two-twenty?"

"Something like that," I grumbled.

"Great," she said, standing up and strapping her pack to her dog's harness. "I'll carry you."

My head snapped up. "Wait, what? I don't need you to carry me."

Her jaw tightened. "We're half a click from an abandoned cabin. The storm's getting worse, and I'm not arguing about this."

I opened my mouth to protest, but the glare she shot me was colder than the rain. Before I could get another word out, she crouched and, with surprising ease, hoisted me onto her back.

I let out a stunned breath as she adjusted her grip, her movements smooth and efficient. The Chinook took the lead, guiding us through the uneven terrain like this was just another day at the office.

I noticed a slight hitch in her step—carrying my weight couldn't have been easy—but she didn't falter. She moved with a steady determination that left me speechless. And, yeah, more than a little humbled.

"Do this often?" I muttered, my pride taking a hit as I clung to her shoulders.

"More than you'd think," she said, shifting me on her back with an effortlessness that made my ego ache. "Though I usually get fewer complaints and less dead weight."

I huffed a breath against her damp shoulder. "Dead weight? I was trying to make your job easier."

"Uh-huh." Her tone was dry, but I thought she might be smiling. "Keep telling yourself that."

A low chuckle escaped me despite the storm, the pain, and my bruised ego. "You don't pull any punches, do you?"

"Not my style," she said, carefully navigating the muddy ground. "Though I'll give you credit—you're easily top three for heaviest rescue."

I lifted a brow. "Top three?" My voice carried mock indignation. "Should I be flattered or offended?"

She chuckled, her grip tightening around my legs as she pushed forward. "Let's just say you've made an impression."

SAM

I readjusted Ryan's weight across my shoulders, trying to distribute it more evenly. The rain slammed down, ice-cold and merciless, but I was too focused to care. My eyes stayed fixed on the muddy path ahead, each step measured and deliberate.

I'd hauled heavier bodies through worse terrain before. The mud sucked at my boots like desert sand, each step a fight against the earth itself. My muscles screamed in protest, and my legs burned with a familiar ache. Then the memories hit, uninvited and raw.

Blistering heat, swallowing me whole. The weight of my squadmate over my shoulders, his uniform soaked with blood and sweat. Mortar fire shaking the ground, dust clouds swallowing the sky. Every breath clogged my throat with grit. The desperate shouts of my unit ringing in my ears. I had to keep moving. Had to get him out.

Ryan shifted slightly against me, and I was yanked back to the present like a slap to the face. Cold rain replaced scorching sun. The only sound was the downpour and our staggered breaths. But my heart was still hammering. My grip on him tightened, but my hands wouldn't stop trembling.

"Sam?" His voice cut through the haze, low and steady. "You good?"

I didn't answer immediately, my jaw locking as I forced myself to keep moving. The cabin wasn't far. Just a few more steps. I could feel Ryan's arm pressing against my shoulder, steady despite the storm, and I knew he could feel the way my pulse was racing.

"Sam," he tried again, softer this time. "Your heart's going a mile a minute. Are you—"

"I'm fine." The words snapped out sharper than I intended, but I didn't apologize. If I let him push, if I let myself crack, I wasn't sure I'd be able to put the pieces back together.

And I hated that. Hated that I wasn't holding it together as well as I should have.

The cabin finally loomed ahead, its dark outline cutting through the rain. Relief flared hot in my chest, but the knots in my stomach didn't ease. I couldn't let the past get in my head. Not when I had a job to finish.

"This is as far as I can carry you," I said, brushing damp hair from my face. My voice was steady now. Controlled. "You'll need to hop up the steps. Think you can manage?"

Ryan's voice was tight, but he nodded. "I'll manage."

I stopped before the porch steps, adjusting my stance before lowering Ryan as carefully as possible. The second his boots hit the ground, I stepped back, rolling my shoulders to shake off the ghost of weight clinging to me.

I hovered next to him as he braced himself against the railing and shifted his weight onto his good leg. Each small hop sent a flicker of pain across his face, but he swallowed it down. Stubborn.

"Take it slow," I muttered, my hand hovering near his back. "Last thing I need is you faceplanting in the doorway."

A dry huff of laughter escaped him as he steadied himself at the top step. "You'd never let me live that down, would you?"

I smirked. "Not a chance."

The cabin stood like a relic of another time—weathered, battered, but still holding on. The loose shutters rattled against the storm, their hollow clatter swallowed by the wind. The porch sagged slightly, but the roof held. That was enough.

Inside, the air was thick with dust and the scent of long-forgotten fires. Two worn chairs slumped next to a stone hearth that dominated one wall, their fabric torn and stuffing exposed, like they'd given up long ago.

I maneuvered Ryan into one of the chairs, steadying him as the old wood groaned under his weight. He exhaled sharply, shifting in discomfort. "Cozy," he muttered.

A smirk tugged at my lips. "Hey, beats drowning in a ravine, right?"

Ryan let out a low chuckle, some of the tension easing from his shoulders. The storm was still howling outside, rain hammering against the roof, but inside—inside, we were safe.

Dropping to my knees in front of the fireplace, I pulled out my waterproof kindling and fire starter out of my coat pocket, my hands moving on muscle memory alone. A small flame flickered within seconds, hungrily licking at the dry wood. I coaxed the kindling gently, tending it until the fire caught and spread, pushing back against the chill in the air.

I turned to Chance, freeing my pack from his harness and placing it by the fire. "Time to rest those weary paws, you drowned rat," I said softly, scratching his ears. He answered with a satisfied grunt, gave one good shake to rid himself of raindrops, and then settled onto the blanket I'd laid out for him.

My eyes drifted to Ryan. He slumped in his chair, teeth clenched, shifting uncomfortably. The rain had soaked him through, his clothes sticking to his frame and dark hair dripping steadily onto his shoulders. The dancing firelight only emphasized the weariness etched across his features.

I grabbed an emergency blanket, a bottle of water, and a protein bar from my pack, then crossed the room. "Here,"

I said, pressing them into his hands. "Eat something. I'll deal with your ankle in a minute."

Ryan accepted the items without protest, peeling open the wrapper as his gaze followed me. I could feel him watching—not with skepticism or impatience, but with something quieter. Something thoughtful.

The weight of my utility belt hit the chair with a dull thud, my fingers already working the clasps of my rain-soaked jacket. I peeled it off, the cold air hitting my skin like a slap, but I barely noticed. Without hesitation, I grabbed the hem of my shirt and tugged it over my head, tossing it aside. The black sports bra underneath was dry enough; that was all that mattered.

There was no point in shivering through wet clothes when we had shelter and fire.

Across the room, Ryan stilled.

I caught the flicker in his gaze, how his body went rigid—not in embarrassment or discomfort, but in something heavier. I didn't have to follow his line of sight to know what he was staring at.

The scars.

I'd stopped thinking about them a long time ago. They weren't secrets, and I sure as hell didn't hide them. Raised, jagged lines across my shoulder, trailing down my

arm—permanent reminders of battles fought and survived.

I didn't acknowledge his staring; I just kept moving, un-
fastening my soaked cargo pants and stepping out of them.
By the time I looked up again, Ryan's eyes had darted away,
his jaw tight, his hands gripping the blanket I'd given him
like he wasn't sure what to do with himself.

But when his gaze flicked back—when he actually
saw—I felt the shift in the air.

His breath hitched. His fingers twitched against the fabric of the blanket.

The firelight danced across the metal of my prosthetic,
casting a soft glow where my lower leg should have been.

His stunned silence stretched between us, thick enough
to choke on.

"You—" His voice cracked. He swallowed hard and
tried again. "You carried me... with *that*?"

I exhaled through my nose, shaking out my pants before
draping them over the back of the chair. "Yeah, Anderson," I said evenly. "I carried you with *that*."

The disbelief was written all over his face like he was
trying to piece together the last hour—how I'd climbed
through the mud, hoisted him onto my back, and hauled
his stubborn ass through the storm—all while wearing a
prosthesis.

Like I hadn't done it before. Like I hadn't been doing it for years.

He opened his mouth, closed it, then scrubbed a hand over his jaw. He looked like he wanted to say something, but whatever it was, it got lost somewhere between his thoughts and his pride.

I sighed, grabbing a dry shirt and pants from my pack and pulling them on, the warmth of the fabric a welcome relief against my chilled skin. "It's a prosthesis, Ryan," I said, voice level. "Not a handicap."

I turned to him, arms crossed, meeting his lingering wide-eyed look with a raised brow. "*Now*, are you going to sit there gawking, or are you going to strip before you freeze to death?"

Chapter Two

♥

SAM

He exhaled sharply, clearly debating whether to argue, but then muttered, "Fine. But only because you're right about the hypothermia thing."

"Smart man," I quipped, rummaging through my pack for another emergency blanket. I tossed in his direction and crossed my arms, waiting.

Ryan hesitated. His gaze flicked around the tiny cabin like it might suddenly offer him privacy. When it didn't, he muttered something and stripped off his soaked jacket and shirt. The cold hit him immediately—his skin pricked with goosebumps, muscles twitching from the chill.

I didn't look away. I'd seen plenty of men undress in the field—usually under worse conditions. My gaze stayed clinical as I assessed him, cataloging the early signs of cold exposure. "Pants too," I said simply.

His jaw ticked, but he obeyed, peeling off his pants with a grimace. Now down to his black boxers, he sat back, looking about as comfortable as a caged animal.

"Happy now?" he muttered, arms crossing over his broad chest.

"Ecstatic," I deadpanned, shaking out the reflective blanket. I wrapped it around his shoulders, tucking it in with quick, practiced movements. The fire's glow flickered across his damp skin, and I caught the way his gaze flicked briefly to the scars on my arms. He didn't ask about them, and I didn't offer.

"This'll keep you warm," I said, already moving toward his ankle.

His ankle was already swollen, angry-looking. When I pressed lightly along the joint, his whole body tensed.

"Sorry," I muttered, my voice softer now. "Good news is, it's not broken. Bad news? It's sprained."

He let out a humorless laugh. "Yeah, I figured that out when I tried to climb out of that ravine."

I didn't respond, already reaching for the roll of bandages in my pack. Silence settled between us as I wrapped his ankle—efficient, steady. This was second nature, something my hands knew how to do without thinking. Still, I felt his eyes on me, watching. Not in that wary way people did when they didn't trust me to know what I was doing. No, this was different.

"Thank you," Ryan said, his voice breaking the quiet.

I glanced up, meeting his gaze. It was steady and sincere. Something tightened in my chest, something I refused to name. Instead, I gave him a single nod. "Just doing my job."

But even I wasn't sure that was the truth.

I finished securing the bandage and pushed to my feet, brushing my hands off on my pants. "Stay put," I ordered, back to business. "I'm going to rig something to collect water. We might be here longer than expected."

RYAN

The warmth of the fire finally started to sink into my bones, chasing away the deep chill that had settled in. I adjusted the blanket around my shoulders, letting out a slow breath as my muscles unknotted one by one. My ankle still throbbed like hell, and my pride? That was taking a big hit.

From my spot near the fire, I glanced at Chance. The dog had curled up in front of the flames, his thick coat glowing in the flickering light. But he wasn't resting, he was watching me. Studying me.

I met his stare, narrowing my eyes. "What?"

Chance didn't blink.

I shifted under his scrutiny. "Don't look at me like that. I didn't *ask* to be carried here, you know."

The dog huffed through his nose and lowered his head to his paws, but his sharp, intelligent gaze never wavered.

I let out a dry chuckle, shaking my head. "Great. Now even the dog's judging me."

Chance's ears twitched, and I swore I caught a flicker of amusement in his expression.

"Yeah, yeah, I get it," I muttered. "You think I'm helpless. Newsflash, buddy—I could've handled this myself. I just... slipped. Mudslides happen."

Chance tilted his head slightly, utterly unimpressed.

I exhaled sharply, rubbing a hand down my face. "Oh, come on! You think this is easy for me? Being carried by *her*?" I gestured toward the door where Sam had disappeared. "Not that she's not impressive. She is. *Insanely* so. But still. A guy's got his pride, you know?"

Chance let out a long, suffering sigh and turned his head away. If dogs could roll their eyes, I was pretty damn sure I'd just witnessed it.

A reluctant smirk tugged at my lips. "You're just as smug as she is, aren't you? A furry little sidekick with an attitude."

The dog lifted his head slightly, giving me a look that screamed, *Are you done yet?*

I shook my head, leaning back into the chair with a quiet laugh. "Fine. You win. Happy now?"

Chance didn't move; he just settled deeper into his spot with that same self-satisfied air. I huffed another laugh, tension I hadn't realized I was still holding finally starting to ebb.

The cabin door creaked open, and Sam stepped back inside, shaking the rain from her hair.

"Storm's still coming down hard," she said, brushing damp strands from her face. "No chance of heading out tonight."

Sam crouched by her pack, digging out a water bottle. She took a long sip before setting it aside, then pulled out a small, neatly folded black T-shirt. Holding it out to me, she kept her tone brisk. "This is all I've got. It's dry. Better than nothing."

I took it, unfolding the fabric, only to pause as I held it up. The damn thing was tiny. I arched a brow. "No offense, but I think I'll stick with the blanket. Besides, I run hot. I'll survive."

Sam shrugged. "Suit yourself. But don't come crying to me if you wake up shivering."

Sam grabbed a few logs from the small stack near the door and fed them into the fire. Then she unrolled a sleeping bag from her pack and spread it out in front of the fire, smoothing it down. She surveyed her work with a nod of satisfaction.

"Alright," she announced, brushing her hands on her pants. "Fire's good and should keep us warm enough for the night."

I raised an eyebrow, still wrapped in the emergency blanket. "Us?"

"Body heat," she replied flatly, reaching for another blanket. "Unless you want to spend the night freezing in that chair. And trust me, I'm not dragging your hypothermic ass out of here in the morning."

My mouth opened to argue, but I shut it just as fast. My gaze flicked to the bedding. "Guess I don't have a choice," I muttered, pushing myself up on my good leg. Hobbling toward the blankets, I eased down with a wince.

Chance padded over, his sharp eyes locked on me like he was assessing my every move. He sat beside Sam, straight-backed and serious, looking an awful lot like he was deciding whether or not I belonged.

I exhaled. "What's with the look?"

Chance didn't blink.

I narrowed my eyes at him. "If you're trying to figure out my intentions, I'll have you know they're completely honorable."

The dog tilted his head slightly, his intelligent gaze unwavering.

I flapped a hand toward the fire. "Look, I just want to get warm, alright?"

Sam looked up from adjusting her blanket, amusement flickering in her eyes. "He's appointed himself trouble detector."

I let out a dramatic scoff, dropping onto the bedding with mock offense. "Me, trouble? I'm practically a saint."

Chance's tail thumped against the floor in a slow, deliberate rhythm—judgmental as hell.

Sam snorted, amusement breaking through her stoic mask. "He's smarter than most people I know. And smug about it, too."

Shaking my head, I let out an unwilling chuckle. "Great. Now I've got *both* of you judging me."

Chapter Three

♥

SAM

The rain drummed steadily against the cabin roof, the only sound filling the silence between us.

Ryan exhaled, tilting his head toward me. "So how long have you been doing this? Search and Rescue, I mean."

I considered my answer momentarily, not altogether comfortable talking about myself. "Long enough. Got out of the military five years ago. Chance and I trained together after that."

Ryan nodded, letting that sink in. "Makes sense. You've got the precision, the focus."

I raised a brow. "Is that a compliment?"

"An observation," he countered smoothly.

Ryan hesitated, then met my gaze. "Can I ask how it happened?"

I didn't answer right away. My fingers traced the edge of the blanket, weighing the question, deciding if I had it in me to tell it again. "You mean my leg?"

He nodded. "Yeah. I mean, if you don't want to talk about it—"

"It's fine," I cut in, surprised by my willingness to share. "Afghanistan. I was in a convoy with my unit. We were delivering supplies to a forward operating base when we hit an IED."

The fire flickered before me, but my mind was miles away, trapped in a memory I could never quite shake.

"Everything was chaos," I continued. "The blast flipped our vehicle. I don't remember much after that—just the heat, the noise, and the pain." I swallowed hard, my jaw tightening. "I was lucky. Some of my team... they didn't make it."

Ryan didn't move or say anything immediately, but when he finally spoke, his voice was quiet, steady. "I'm sorry, Sam. That's..." he exhaled, shaking his head slightly. "No one should have to go through that."

I nodded, my expression unreadable. "There were times I didn't think I'd get back on my feet—literally or otherwise. But I'm stubborn, and I had something to prove. To myself, mostly."

I glanced at him, the weight of those months, those years, pressing against my ribs. "I wasn't going to let it define me. So, I found a way to keep doing what I love. Search and Rescue was a natural fit."

Ryan sat quietly, letting my words settle. He was trying to picture it, I could tell. But he couldn't. Not really.

Shifting against my bedroll, I watched the fire dance. "So, Anderson, what's your story? How'd you end up in Search and Rescue?"

His expression grew thoughtful. "My dad, actually. He was a Coast Guard rescue swimmer. I grew up with stories about him saving people when everyone else said it couldn't be done. Wanted to live up to that, you know? Make that kind of difference."

I nodded, absorbing that. "Sounds like he made an impression."

"Yeah, he did," Ryan admitted, his gaze fixed on the fire. "But he was gone a lot. Work always came first. It wasn't until I got older that I realized... he was running from something. Guess that's why I never settled down. Didn't want to be like that—always leaving."

For a beat, neither of us spoke. The logs in the fireplace crackled, sending flickering light across the cabin walls.

Outside, the rain had softened to a steady rhythm, no longer the violent downpour from earlier.

I shifted slightly, adjusting the blanket around me as the fire crackled, casting flickering shadows against the cabin walls. Across from me, Ryan lay back, his jaw tight, the tension in his face betraying the pain in his injured ankle. He hadn't complained about it, not once, but I saw the way he gritted his teeth every time he moved.

A long moment passed between us, filled only by the steady patter of rain on the roof and the occasional pop of burning wood. Finally, I broke the silence. "I need to take off my leg."

Ryan's gaze flicked to me, steady and unreadable. "Your prosthetic?"

I smirked, tilting my head. "No, my other leg," I deadpanned. "Yes, my prosthetic, Anderson. I don't usually sleep with it on unless I have to. But if it's going to make you uncomfortable—"

"Why would it?" he cut in, his voice even. He shifted slightly, sucking in a breath at the movement. "You think something like that would bother me after everything we've been through today?"

I studied him, searching for hesitation, but found none. Just calm certainty, like it was the most natural thing in the world. Satisfied, I nodded and leaned back, removing the prosthetic with the same practiced ease I'd done for years.

"You'd be surprised," I said, setting it aside. "Some people don't know how to handle it. They either act like it's this huge deal or pretend it doesn't exist. Both get exhausting."

Ryan didn't flinch, didn't shift uncomfortably. He just watched me like he had earlier—taking in every part of me, scars and all, without looking away. "Well, I'm not some people," he said, his voice softer now. "You're the one who carried me out of that ravine, Sam. Trust me, I'm not going to sit here and get weird about a prosthetic leg."

A ghost of a smile pulled at my lips. I pulled the blanket over my lap, letting the warmth sink in. "Good to know."

Ryan hesitated for a beat. "Does it hurt?"

I kept my eyes on the fire. "Not really. Well, not now, anyway. Get these weird ghost pains sometimes, like my foot's still there having a fit. You learn to deal with it."

He nodded, absorbing that. "Couldn't have been easy, getting used to everything."

I exhaled, scratching absently behind Chance's ears. "You adapt, or you don't. Simple as that."

Ryan was quiet for a long moment before finally saying, "For what it's worth, you're tougher than just about anyone I've ever met."

A rough chuckle escaped me. "I'll take that as a compliment. Coming from you, that's saying something."

"Good night, Monroe," Ryan murmured, his voice quieter now, almost warm.

I hesitated just a second before replying, "Good night, Anderson."

As the rain softened outside, I let my head rest against the rolled-up edge of my blanket, the sound of the fire lulling me into something dangerously close to peace.

RYAN

The fire crackled, casting warm light across the cabin, but sleep refused to come. I lay there, staring at the ceiling, hyperaware of everything—the heat from the fire, the storm still whispering outside, and most of all, the woman sleeping next to me.

I felt every time she shifted under the blanket, even the slightest movement. The subtle brush of her body against mine sent my pulse into overdrive.

I squeezed my eyes shut, willing my thoughts elsewhere. This wasn't the time. It sure as hell wasn't the place. But my body had its own damn ideas, heat curling low in my stomach as my mind betrayed me with images I had no business entertaining.

Sam peeling off her shirt with efficient, no-nonsense movements. The way the firelight had caught on the sleek muscles in her arms, the curve of her collarbone. The scars that mapped across her skin, not imperfections but stories—proof of everything she'd endured and come out the other side stronger. She moved like she carried the weight of the world, and somehow, she still stood tall.

The memory of her carrying me through the storm flashed through my mind, and my chest tightened. I wasn't a small man. But she'd done it like it was nothing, her body stronger than it looked, moving with practiced confidence.

I swallowed hard, watching the firelight flickering over her face. A loose strand of hair had fallen across her cheek, and my fingers twitched with the urge to brush it back. My gaze drifted lower, following the smooth line of her neck and the way her pulse beat steadily beneath her skin. I imagined pressing my lips there, learning her taste, following the delicate slope down to her collarbone.

I exhaled sharply and clenched my fists. Get it together, Anderson.

Sam shifted in her sleep, murmuring something incoherent, and before I could react, she rolled toward me.

Her head came to rest against my chest, her body curling instinctively into the warmth beside her. One arm draped across my torso, her fingers resting against my ribs, sending heat spiraling through me.

I went completely still, barely breathing.

Her hair tickled my chin, her scent—mint, rain, something uniquely her—wrapping around me, making it impossible to think straight. I could feel the steady rise and fall of her breathing, the way her body fit against mine, how damn right it felt even though I knew it shouldn't.

I tried to focus on something else, but my body had already decided how it felt about this situation, and fuck—this was torture. The kind I wasn't sure I wanted to escape.

Slowly, carefully, I tried to shift away without waking her. But the moment I moved, she let out a soft noise of protest, nuzzling closer. Her hand slid against my chest, fingers brushing over my skin.

A sharp jolt shot through me, my breath catching in my throat.

Jesus. This was going to be a long night.

Sam's fingers continued to skim down over my stomach in her sleep, featherlight but enough to send a sharp pulse of heat through me. My breath hitched, muscles tensing involuntarily at the sensation.

This was bad.

She didn't even realize what she was doing, her touch unintentional. But my body didn't give a damn. Every nerve was locked onto the slow drag of her fingertips, the warmth of her palm against my skin.

I clenched my jaw, breathing through the rush of need clawing its way up my spine. I had to stop this before I lost my mind completely.

With more control than I thought I had, I caught her wrist mid-motion, stilling her hand before it could wander any lower.

"Sam," I rasped, my voice rough. I nudged her shoulder gently. "Wake up."

Her lashes fluttered, a sleepy frown pulling at her lips as she stirred. Awareness crept in slowly, her body shifting against mine. Then her gaze found mine—still hazy, still soft—before dropping to where our bodies had tangled together during the night.

Her breath caught.

I saw the moment understanding dawned, the heat rising to her cheeks as she started pulling away.

"I—" She cleared her throat, her voice barely above a murmur. "I didn't mean to—"

My hand tightened instinctively around her wrist, stopping her retreat. "Don't," I whispered, the word slipping out before I could think better of it.

Her eyes widened slightly, catching the firelight. For once, that carefully constructed wall of hers cracked, and I could see the uncertainty beneath—and something else. Something that made my pulse quicken.

"Ryan." My name fell from her lips like a question, her body still half-pressed against mine, our faces inches apart.

I should have let her go. Should have made a joke, eased the tension, given us both an out. But I couldn't bring myself to do it. Not when she looked at me like that, her usual composure slipping just enough to reveal the passionate woman beneath.

"I know this is crazy," I murmured, my voice rougher than intended. "We just met. But I can't stop thinking about you." The confession hung between us, heavy with intent.

Sam's breath hitched, her eyes darkening as they searched mine. She didn't move away, didn't break the contact where our bodies pressed together. Instead, her fingers curled slightly against my skin, her touch deliberate now.

"This is a bad idea," she whispered, but her words lacked conviction.

"Probably," I agreed, my thumb tracing slow circles on her wrist where I still held her. "Tell me to stop."

She swallowed, and I watched the movement in her throat, mesmerized. "I should," she murmured.

"But you won't," I finished for her, my voice barely audible over the crackle of the fire.

Something shifted in her expression—doubt giving way to decision. Her gaze dropped to my mouth, lingering there with an intensity that made heat pool low in my stomach.

"Screw it," she breathed.

Then her lips were on mine, and everything else disappeared.

The kiss was nothing like I expected—not tentative or questioning, but fierce. Demanding. Her mouth moved against mine with the same determined focus she brought to everything, like she'd made up her mind and wouldn't be swayed.

I groaned into her mouth, my hand sliding up to cup the back of her neck, fingers threading through her hair. She tasted like warmth and something wild—untamed and unapologetic. My other arm wrapped around her waist, pulling her flush against me, the heat of her body searing through the thin layers between us.

Sam made a soft sound in the back of her throat, something between a sigh and a moan, and the sound shot straight through me. Her hands were suddenly everywhere—tracing the lines of my shoulders, sliding down my chest, fingertips brushing against the waistband of my boxers.

"Sam," I breathed against her lips, my voice strained with restraint. "Are you sure about this?"

She answered by kissing me harder, her teeth grazing my bottom lip. My breath caught as she shifted, straddling me in one fluid motion. Her weight settled against me, and I groaned at the contact, my hands instinctively gripping her hips. She looked down at me, hair tousled and lips swollen, the most beautiful thing I'd ever seen.

"Does that answer your question?" she murmured, her voice low and husky.

"Crystal clear," I managed.

The firelight cast shadows across her face, highlighting the sharp angles of her cheekbones, the determined set of her jaw. But her eyes held me captive—dark and intent, watching me with a hunger that matched my own.

She rolled her hips experimentally, and my head fell back against the makeshift bedding, a curse hissing through my teeth. The friction was maddening, even through layers of fabric. My hands tightened on her hips, guiding her movements as she rocked against me again, more deliberate this time.

"You're killing me," I rasped, watching her through half-lidded eyes. The sight of her above me, backlit by firelight, was almost too much to bear.

Her lips curved into a subtle smile—not quite smug, but knowing. She leaned down, her mouth brushing against my jaw, then trailing lower to my neck. Her teeth grazed the sensitive skin there, followed by the soothing press of her tongue. Each touch sent sparks shooting down my spine.

Chapter Four

♥

SAM

"I need to taste you," Ryan growled. His eyes met mine, dark with hunger, as he gripped my hips with renewed intensity. In one fluid motion, he flipped our positions, careful of his injured ankle, but still managing to press me into the bedding with his weight. The sudden shift made my breath catch, a thrill racing through me at the controlled strength in his movements.

"Your ankle," I murmured, concern briefly cutting through the haze of desire.

"Don't care," he said roughly, his mouth already trailing down my neck. "Worth it."

His hands slid beneath my shirt, calloused palms against my bare skin, sending electricity through my veins. When his mouth reached the edge of my sports bra, he paused, eyes flicking up to mine in silent question.

I nodded, breath shallow as I helped him tug the fabric over my head. The cool air hit my exposed skin, but Ryan's gaze burned hotter than the fire crackling beside us. His eyes darkened, taking in every inch of me with an intensity that made my pulse race.

"You're incredible," he murmured thick with desire.

I wasn't used to this—being seen, being wanted so openly. My body had always been a tool, functional rather than beautiful. But the way Ryan looked at me, touched me—like I was something precious—made my chest tight with something I couldn't name. Something that scared me more than anything I'd faced before.

When his lips closed around my nipple, my back arched off the bedding, a gasp tearing from my throat. His tongue circled the sensitive peak, teeth grazing just enough to send sparks shooting through me. His hand moved to my other breast, thumb brushing over the sensitive peak as his mouth continued its sweet torture. Each caress was deliberate, unhurried—as if he had all the time in the world to learn my body.

I wasn't used to this kind of attention, this focused pleasure. My relationships had always been quick, convenient—necessary releases rather than explorations. But Ryan touched me like he was memorizing me.

"Ryan," I breathed, my fingers threading through his hair.

He hummed against my skin, the vibration sending another wave of pleasure through me. His hand slid down my stomach, fingers dipping beneath the waistband of my pants. He paused there, looking up at me with eyes dark with desire but still waiting—still asking permission.

I lifted my hips in answer, helping him slide the fabric down my legs.

His mouth continued its journey downward, mapping the planes of my stomach, pausing to trace the scars that marked my body. Where I expected hesitation, there was only reverence—each kiss pressed to damaged skin a silent acceptance of everything I'd survived.

My throat tightened with unexpected emotion. I was used to lovers avoiding my scars, treating them as things to overlook. But Ryan touched them deliberately, his lips lingering.

When his mouth reached the waistband of my underwear, I shivered, anticipation coiling tight in my belly. His fingers hooked into the sides, slowly sliding the fabric down.

"Beautiful," he murmured, his voice a rough caress.

I wasn't used to vulnerability, to being laid bare like this. My instinct was to deflect, to take control back. But something in his expression—hungry, intense, appreciative—kept me still, breath caught in my throat.

He settled between my thighs, his broad shoulders pushing them wider. Seeing him there, looking up at me with those dark eyes, sent a pulse of heat through me. His breath ghosted over my sensitive skin, and my fingers curled into the bedding.

"I need to taste you," he said again, his voice a low rumble that vibrated through me. "I've been thinking about this since I first saw you."

I couldn't form words, could only nod as his mouth descended. The first touch of his tongue against me tore a gasp from my throat, my hips lifting involuntarily. His hands gripped my thighs, holding me open as he explored me.

His tongue worked against me with the same confident skill that had defined everything else about him. Each stroke was purposeful, finding all the places that made my breath hitch and my body tense. My fingers threaded through his hair, holding him closer as pleasure built inside me with frightening intensity.

"Ryan," I gasped, the word barely recognizable. My thighs trembled as he slid one finger inside me, then another, curling them in perfect rhythm with his tongue.

My head fell back, eyes closing as I surrendered to the feeling. This wasn't part of the plan—none of this was—but I couldn't bring myself to care anymore.

When he added a third finger, stretching me deliciously while his tongue circled my most sensitive spot, something inside me shattered. The orgasm hit with unexpected force, my back arching sharply off the bedding as waves of pleasure crashed through me. Ryan held me through it, his movements never faltering as he coaxed every tremor from my body.

I was still shaking when he moved back up, his mouth capturing mine in a searing kiss. I could taste myself on his lips, and the intimacy of it sent another aftershock through me. His hardness pressed against my thigh, a reminder of his own need.

"I want you," I whispered against his mouth, my voice raw with honesty I rarely allowed myself.

RYAN

Her words hit me like a physical force, igniting something primal inside me. I kissed her again, deeper this time, swallowing her soft moan as my hand slid up her side.

"I want you too," I breathed, my voice strained with need. "More than I've wanted anything."

Sam's eyes darkened at my confession, her hands sliding down my chest to the waistband of my boxers. Her fingers hooked into the elastic, tugging them down with determined efficiency. I reached down with one hand to help, wincing slightly as the movement jostled my injured ankle.

"Careful," she whispered, her voice gentler than I'd heard it before.

I chuckled, low and rough. "Worth the pain."

My boxers joined the pile of discarded clothing, and Sam's gaze traveled down my body, lingering on my hard cock. Her breath hitched slightly, and I saw the flicker of appreciation in her eyes before she masked it.

"Like what you see?" I murmured, my voice rough with desire.

Sam's lips curved into a slight smile, her fingers wrapping around my length with confident precision. "Maybe," she whispered, her thumb brushing over the sensitive tip. "But I'd like it better inside me."

A groan tore from my throat as her hand stroked me, each movement deliberate and maddening. "Sam," I rasped, my hips jerking into her touch despite the dull throb in my ankle. "You're torturing me."

She leaned up to capture my mouth in another searing kiss, her tongue sliding against mine as her hand continued its delicious rhythm. When she finally pulled back, her eyes were dark with need, her breathing uneven.

"Condom?" she asked, ever practical even in this moment.

I shook my head, frustration creeping in. "I wasn't planning on getting stranded in a cabin with an irresistible woman during a rescue."

Sam's lips quirked, her hand never ceasing its maddening rhythm. "Lucky for you, I'm always prepared."

She pulled away from me, and I nearly groaned at the loss of contact. But then she was leaning over to her pack, rummaging through a side pocket with that same efficient purpose she brought to everything. When she returned, she held a small foil packet between her fingers.

"Standard issue?" I asked, my voice rough with desire and amusement. I took the condom from her and sat back on my heels to roll it down my length.

Sam's eyes followed my movements, her lips curving into that subtle smirk. "Search and Rescue 101. Always be prepared for anything."

"Anything, huh?" I echoed, my voice dropping lower as I moved back over her. My hands slid beneath her thighs, lifting them to wrap around my waist. The position pressed my cock against her entrance, hot and ready, and we both groaned at the contact.

"Ryan," she breathed, her hands gripping my shoulders. "Stop teasing."

I leaned down, my lips brushing against hers as I positioned myself. "Yes, ma'am."

With one smooth thrust, I pushed inside her, and the world narrowed to just this—the tight heat of her body around mine, the soft gasp that escaped her lips, the way her nails dug into my skin. I stilled, giving her time to adjust to my size, fighting the urge to move. The sensation of being inside her was overwhelming—tight, hot, perfect. Her eyes were locked on mine, pupils dilated with desire, lips parted as she breathed through the initial stretch.

"Move," she commanded, voice husky and raw.

I didn't need to be told twice. I withdrew slowly before sliding back in, establishing a rhythm that had us both gasping. Each thrust drove me deeper, her body yielding to mine in a way that felt like coming home. Her legs tightened around my waist, changing the angle and drawing a groan from deep in my chest.

The cabin filled with the sounds of our breathing, the crackle of the fire, and the storm still raging outside. We created our own rhythm—urgent yet controlled, each movement building the tension coiling between us.

"Harder," Sam gasped, her fingers tangling in my hair, pulling me down for a kiss that was all desperate need.

I obliged, driving into her with renewed intensity, careful of my injured ankle but unwilling to hold back. The pain was there, dull and distant, but it couldn't compete with the pleasure coursing through me.

Sam's body responded to every thrust, meeting me halfway, her hips lifting to take me deeper. There was nothing hesitant about the way she moved, nothing shy in her reactions. Her confidence, her raw desire, only fueled my own.

"You feel so good," I groaned against her neck, my teeth grazing the sensitive skin there. "So perfect."

She slid one hand between our bodies, fingers finding her clit with practiced precision. The sight of her touching herself while I moved inside her nearly undid me—her confidence, her willingness to take her pleasure, was the most erotic thing I'd ever witnessed. Her fingers moved in tight, deliberate circles, perfectly timed with my thrusts.

"God, Sam," I groaned, my rhythm faltering as I watched her.

The intensity in her eyes stole my breath. She wasn't looking away—she was watching me watch her, taking in my reaction with a heat that matched the fire beside us. Her lips parted, breath coming in short gasps as her fingers worked faster.

"Close," she whispered, her voice breaking on the word. "I'm so close."

I shifted my weight, changing the angle of my thrusts to hit deeper. Her back arched off the bedding, a strangled moan escaping her throat. I could feel her tightening around me, her body tensing as she approached the edge.

"Let go," I urged, my voice strained with the effort of holding back my own release. "I've got you."

Something in my words seemed to break her final restraint. Sam's body went rigid beneath me, her inner walls clenching around me as she came. The sight of her coming undone—head thrown back, lips parted on a silent cry, cheeks flushed with pleasure—pushed me over the edge. My own orgasm tore through me, each pulse of pleasure more intense than the last.

I collapsed beside her, careful not to crush her with my weight, my chest heaving as I struggled to catch my breath. For a long moment, neither of us spoke. The only sounds were our ragged breathing and the steady patter of rain against the cabin roof.

Sam lay beside me, her body still trembling with aftershocks. When I finally turned to look at her, her eyes were closed, lips slightly parted as she caught her breath. She looked different in the firelight with her guard down and her usual composure stripped away. Softer somehow, yet still unmistakably strong.

I reached out, brushing a strand of hair from her face. Her eyes opened at the touch, meeting mine with an expression I couldn't quite read. For a moment, vulnerability flickered there—something open and unguarded—before her usual composure slid back into place.

"Well," she murmured, her voice still husky from exertion, "that's one way to keep warm."

A laugh rumbled through my chest, unexpected and genuine. "Efficient."

Her lips curved into a small smile, something softer than her usual smirk. "Efficiency is important."

I reached for the discarded blanket, pulling it over our cooling bodies. Sam shifted, her back pressed against my chest as I wrapped an arm around her waist. The moment's intimacy wasn't lost on me—how easily she fit against me, how natural it felt to hold her like this.

"We should get some sleep," Sam murmured, her voice thick with exhaustion. "Storm might break by morning."

I nuzzled into her neck, breathing in her scent. "You're right." My voice was rough with exhaustion, but I couldn't quite bring myself to close my eyes. Not yet. Not when having her in my arms felt this good.

Sam's breathing gradually slowed, her body relaxing against mine as sleep claimed her. I stayed awake a little longer, watching the firelight play across her skin, memorizing the feel of her against me.

Tomorrow, we'd have to figure out what this meant—if it meant anything at all. Tomorrow, we'd be back to reality, back to our separate worlds. But for now, in this moment, with the storm outside and the warmth between us, nothing else mattered.

I gently kissed her shoulder and finally let my eyes close, sleep pulling me under with unexpected ease.

Chapter Five

♥

RYAN

Morning light streamed through the worn slats of the cabin, cutting golden stripes across the floor. The steady sound of rain against the roof had softened from last night's storm, a gentle rhythm that blended with the quiet crackle of dying embers in the fireplace.

Beside me, Sam remained still, her breathing slow and deep. Chance lay curled at her feet, ears flicking at the subtle creaks of the old cabin.

Sam shifted, stretching slightly before her eyes blinked open, hazy with sleep. "Morning," she murmured, voice rough and unguarded.

"Morning," I echoed, my own voice quieter than usual. "Storm's let up."

She stretched again, the movement languid and easy, muscles flexing beneath her skin. "How's the ankle?"

I shifted position, biting back a groan as pain shot through me, still hot and persistent but not as bad as yesterday. "Still attached."

She sat up and reached for her prosthetic with practiced ease. Rising, she crossed to the dying fire and tossed on a few sticks, waiting for the flames to catch before grabbing her clothes.

"We'll need to rig something for you to walk with," she said, already thinking ahead. "Can't exactly carry you all the way back."

I exhaled, shifting slightly on the bedroll. "Yeah, I think I've had enough of being hauled around for one trip."

She glanced over her shoulder, eyes narrowing—but I caught the slight twitch at the corner of her lips before she turned away.

As Sam stepped outside with Chance at her side, I leaned back, listening to the steady drizzle drumming against the roof. The sound filled the quiet space, underscoring just how damn useless I felt sitting here while she handled everything. I wasn't used to being the one stuck on the sidelines.

She returned a few minutes later, shaking the droplets from her jacket. "The trail's muddy, but we should manage. I'll find a sturdy branch to make a crutch for you."

"Want me to tag along?" I asked, knowing damn well what the answer would be but hating how useless I felt.

Sam knelt beside me, her gaze steady, her voice softer than I expected. "Thanks, but I got this."

Sam stood, slinging her pack over her shoulder as she pulled up the hood of her jacket. "I won't be long," she said, giving me one last assessing look, like she was debating whether I'd actually stay put.

Before I could argue, she turned and slipped out the door, her footsteps fading into the steady patter of rain.

Apparently assigned to babysitting duty, Chance padded over and sat beside me, fixing me with a knowing look.

"Well, buddy," I muttered, rubbing the thick fur behind his ears. "Looks like it's just you and me."

I sighed, dragging a hand through my hair. The memories of last night were still fresh, every touch, every breath, still humming beneath my skin. But while my head was caught up in it, Sam seemed to have already locked it away, treating the morning like nothing had changed.

Not a lingering glance. Not a hint of hesitation. Just business as usual.

I frowned, absentmindedly scratching Chance's ears as I replayed it all in my head. Sam didn't seem awkward or regretful and she didn't strike me as the type to second-guess herself. But she also didn't acknowledge what had happened between us, didn't even leave room for a conversation about it. The walls she'd let slip last night were back in place, solid as ever.

And I wasn't sure what to make of that.

I blew out a slow breath, focusing on the more immediate challenge—getting dressed without putting weight on my ankle. My clothes were still draped over the rickety chair near the fireplace, slightly damp but better than nothing.

I glanced at the door, determined to get myself sorted before Sam returned. The last thing I wanted was to give her another reason to see me as helpless.

The rough wooden floor was cool beneath my feet as I tested my weight, gritting my teeth against the sharp protest from my ankle. Every instinct told me to stay off it, but sitting around wasn't an option. With slow, measured steps, I hobbled toward the chair where my clothes lay.

I reached for my shirt first, the fabric still faintly warm from where it had rested near the dying fire. The pants were going to be the real battle.

I propped myself against the wall, wrestling one leg into my pants before tackling the other, cursing under my breath as the fabric caught on my swollen ankle. Each tug and adjustment tested what little patience I had left; the simple act of getting dressed turned into an endurance exercise. By the time I managed to fasten my belt, sweat had begun to bead across my skin.

Steadying myself against the wall, I let out a heavy breath.

The worst part? Sam would take one look at me and know exactly how much effort it had taken.

SAM

I stepped inside just as Ryan finished dressing. The air was still thick with the scent of rain and damp earth, but at least the worst of the storm had passed. I'd found a sturdy branch stripped of excess bark and twigs. It wasn't perfect, but it would do.

"Well, moment of truth," I said, holding it out. "Want to give it a shot?"

Ryan took the makeshift crutch, testing his weight with small, careful steps. He winced slightly but managed to steady himself. "Huh, this might actually work," he said, looking it over with surprise.

His eyes stayed on me a beat too long, but I was already moving, gathering up our bedding and stuffing it into my pack. "Let's go," I said, adjusting my pack straps. "Trail's not getting any better."

Chance stuck close, ears perked as he surveyed the wet ground. Ahead, the trail was a sloppy mess of mud and storm debris, but we'd manage it.

I took point, keeping a steady pace while watching for the best route. Behind me, Ryan's uneven footfalls marked his progress with the crutch.

"Hanging in there?" I called back without turning.

Ryan huffed. "If by 'hanging in there' you mean caked in mud and feeling like dead weight, then sure, I'm fantastic."

I smiled, shaking my head. "Stop being dramatic. You're managing."

"Easy for you to say," he grumbled. "You're not the one hobbling through this swamp."

I stopped and turned to face him, arching a brow. "Want another piggyback ride?" I teased, but the flicker of concern in his eyes didn't escape me.

"No chance," he shot back, shaking his head like the idea pained him.

I shrugged. "Your call. But we need to pick up the pace. We need to make it to the ranger station before the sun sets."

Ryan let out a heavy breath, readjusted his crutch with unsteady hands, and pressed onward. I could sense his eyes when I turned back to the trail ahead. Sure, he'd looked at me before, but this felt different somehow. There was an intensity to it now as if he was seeing me in a whole new light.

Branches dripped overhead, creating a persistent patter that mingled with the squelch of our boots in the mud. I kept my eyes forward, focused on picking the safest path through the debris-strewn trail, but my mind refused to stay as disciplined as my gaze.

Last night kept replaying itself in flashes of sensation—Ryan's calloused hands against my skin, the heat of his mouth trailing down my body, the way he'd looked at me when I came undone beneath him. My body still hummed with the memory, a lingering ache between my thighs reminding me of how he'd filled me so perfectly.

I swallowed hard, forcing my thoughts back to the present. The damp earth. The smell of pine. The weight of my pack against my shoulders. Anything but the way his voice had roughened when he'd whispered my name.

What happened between us had been... unexpected. Intense. Something I hadn't planned for, hadn't even considered until I felt his body against mine. But it was over now. A moment stolen in the storm, nothing more. It couldn't be anything more.

My life didn't have room for complications like this. I kept things simple—my work, my routines, the boundaries I maintained. Ryan Anderson didn't fit into any of that. He was temporary, passing through. And that was fine. That was how it needed to be.

"Sam?" Ryan's voice cut through my thoughts, pulling me back to reality.

I glanced over my shoulder. "Yeah?"

"You're walking like you're trying to leave me behind," he said, a hint of strain in his voice. "Mind slowing down a bit?"

I hadn't realized I'd picked up my pace, too caught up in my head. "Sorry," I muttered, slowing my steps. "Just trying to make good time."

The gentle burble of water led me to a narrow stream winding between the trees.

"Let's take a break," I called back to Ryan, who was making steady but slow progress with his makeshift crutch. "We should rest and refill our water."

Ryan limped over, relief washing across his face as he lowered himself onto a fallen log beside the water. He stretched his injured leg out, grimacing as he rotated his ankle slightly.

Chance padded over and plopped down beside him, his sharp amber eyes locked onto Ryan like he was assessing the damage.

Ryan arched a brow at him. "What's with the look? I'm fine. Just a little banged up."

Chance sighed exaggeratedly, his tail giving a single, unimpressed thump against the damp earth.

I glanced over my shoulder, catching the exchange. "He thinks you're being dramatic."

Ryan scoffed, wiping sweat from his forehead. "Says the guy who didn't take a nosedive down a ravine."

"Chance doesn't fall," I said flatly, unscrewing my bottle cap. "He's too dignified for that."

Ryan let out a low chuckle. "Guess that makes me the clumsy one."

"You said it, not me." I stood and handed him the second water bottle. "Drink. Hydration's your friend."

Ryan took it, his fingers brushing mine for half a second before he twisted off the cap and took a long sip. "Thanks."

I sat on a nearby rock, my gaze drifting over the slow-moving stream. Sunlight filtered through the trees, glinting off the water as it trickled over smooth stones. The air felt fresher down here, the scent of wet earth lingering from the storm. I didn't mind the moment of stillness—not after the night we'd had.

Ryan took his time finishing the water, rolling his shoulders like he was in no hurry to get moving. "You good to keep going?" I asked, slipping my bottle back into my pack.

"Yeah." He exhaled and leaned back slightly but made no immediate effort to stand. "Just enjoying the view for a second."

I followed his gaze toward the horizon, where shafts of golden light cut through the canopy, painting streaks of warmth across the damp forest floor. It was beautiful; I'd give him that. But we weren't out of here yet.

Ryan pushed himself upright, gritting his teeth as his ankle protested. He nodded toward Chance, who had already perked up, ready to move. "Lead the way, buddy."

Chance gave a low huff, his tail wagging as he trotted forward.

I stayed close to Ryan, adjusting my pace to match his. The descent wasn't easy, and every so often, Ryan's crutch sank into the softened earth, forcing him to readjust.

Chance kept an easy lead, occasionally glancing back to check our progress. Smart dog.

"We're about half a mile out from the ranger station," I said, my voice even but laced with relief.

Ryan let out a heavy breath, gripping the crutch tighter. "Good. My ankle's already filing a formal complaint."

The corner of my lips twitched, though I kept my eyes on the trail ahead. "Tell it to hang in there. We're almost done."

Then my boot slid out from under me.

I caught myself hard on one knee, my hands digging into the mud and rocks as pain jolted through my leg. A sharp sting bloomed across my palm.

"Sam!" Ryan's voice cut through the air, sharper than I expected.

"I'm fine," I bit out, already pushing myself upright, ignoring the stiffness in my knee and the sting in my hand. I wasn't about to give him—or anyone—a reason to think I needed saving.

"You're bleeding," Ryan pointed out, nodding toward my scraped palm.

"It's nothing," I muttered, wiping the blood on my pant leg before adjusting my pack. A little scrape wasn't worth stopping over.

Ryan moved closer, his steps uneven but determined. "Let me take your pack."

I turned to him, frowning. "What?"

"Let me carry it," he repeated, calm but firm.

I stared at him, baffled. "I don't need you to carry my pack. I'm fine."

Ryan let out a slow breath, gripping his crutch like he was holding onto his patience. "Sam, you slipped. You're hurt."

I huffed a humorless laugh. "A slip in the mud isn't an injury, Anderson. It happens."

"That's not the point." His voice softened, but the quiet intensity in his gaze didn't waver. "You've been carrying me—literally and figuratively—since yesterday. Let me do something to help."

My jaw tightened, something sharp twisting in my chest. "I've carried a hell of a lot worse."

"I know," he said, and the quiet understanding in those two words nearly knocked the wind out of me.

I turned away, adjusting my pack again as if that would fix the sudden unsteadiness in my chest.

"I don't need your pity," I said, my voice coming out harder than I meant.

"It's not pity," Ryan said, his frustration evident. "It's respect. But you're so damn stubborn you can't see when someone wants to help."

I spun back to face him, eyes narrowing. "I don't need help, Ryan. That's the point. I've spent years proving I don't need anyone to step in and save me."

"And I'm not trying to save you," he shot back, his voice rising slightly. "I'm trying to share the load. There's a difference."

"Not to me," I muttered, already turning back toward the trail. "Let's just keep moving."

Ryan remained where he stood, his expression unreadable. "Is that how it's going to be? After everything?"

I froze, tension coiling between my shoulders. "After what, exactly?" I knew damn well what he meant, but I wasn't ready to acknowledge it. Not here, not like this.

"Last night," he said, his voice quieter now but no less intense. "What happened between us."

I exhaled, my gaze fixed on the muddy ground. "Last night was... last night." My voice softened despite my best efforts to keep it steady. "It was cold, we were stuck. Things happen."

"Things happen," Ryan echoed, disbelief coloring his tone. "Is that all it was to you? Just 'things happening'?"

I met his gaze then, something in his tone drawing my eyes to his. The intensity I found there made my chest tighten.

"I don't do this, Ryan," I said, gesturing vaguely between us. "Whatever this is. I don't have room for it."

"You don't have room," he repeated, voice flat. "Or you don't want to make room?"

"That's neither here nor there," I said, keeping my voice even. "It happened. It was good. End of story."

"End of story," he repeated, a humorless laugh escaping him. "Just like that?"

I turned fully to face him, crossing my arms. "What did you expect, Ryan? That we'd wake up and everything would be different? That one night changed everything?"

His expression hardened, but something else was beneath it, which looked dangerously close to hurt. "I expected you to at least acknowledge it happened. Not shut down and pretend it didn't mean anything."

"Did it?" I challenged, heart hammering against my ribs. "Mean something?"

Ryan's gaze never wavered. "You know it did."

The certainty in his voice felt like a physical blow. I opened my mouth to respond, but the words died on my tongue. What could I say? That he was wrong? That would be a lie, and we both knew it.

"We barely know each other," I finally managed.

"That's not true," Ryan said, shifting his weight against the crutch. "I know you're stubborn as hell. I know you push yourself harder than anyone I've ever met. I know you care about your work, about doing things right." His voice dropped lower. "And I know how you taste, how you feel when you come apart. I know the sounds you make when—"

"Stop," I cut him off, my voice sharp. Heat flooded my cheeks, unwanted and betraying. "That's not what I meant."

"Then what did you mean, Sam?" Ryan's eyes held mine, refusing to let me look away. "Because from where I'm standing, it seems like you're running from something that scares you more than anything you faced in that storm."

I swallowed hard, his words hitting too close to home. "I'm going to check the trail," I said, leaving no room for argument. "You stay put and rest."

Chapter Six

♥

RYAN

I eased onto a fallen log, finally taking the weight off my ankle. Relief was instant, but the ache lingered, a dull reminder of how useless I felt. I adjusted my crutch against the log and rolled my shoulders, trying to shake the tension coiled in them.

Chance sat a few feet away, watching me.

"Well, buddy," I muttered, twisting open my water bottle. "I think I royally screwed up." I took a long drink, the cool water a stark contrast to the heat of frustration burning through me. "She's got walls thicker than a damn fortress."

Chance tilted his head, ears slanting forward.

"Don't look at me like that," I sighed, rubbing my face. "I know what you're thinking—I pushed too hard."

Chance tilted his head slightly, one ear twitching like he was considering the statement.

I chuckled, shaking my head. "Yeah, I know. She doesn't need anyone. Least of all me." The words sat heavy in my chest, and I rubbed the back of my neck, trying to sort through the mess in my head. "But... it's not about need, is it? It's about choosing to let someone in. Even when you think you're better off alone."

Chance let out a small huff, his eyes somehow conveying both judgment and understanding.

"I get it," I said, leaning back. "She's had to fight for everything—to prove herself over and over. The last thing she needs is some guy thinking he can waltz in and fix things." I stared at the muddy ground, water still pooling in the deeper indentations. "But that's not what I want."

The dog's ears perked up slightly, his gaze steady on mine.

"I don't want to fix her," I continued quietly. "I just want to know her. The real her—not just the badass who hauled me out of that ravine."

Chance's tail thumped once against the ground.

"What, you think I've got a shot?" I asked with a dry laugh.

The dog's expression remained enigmatic, eyes fixed on mine with that uncanny intelligence. His tail gave one more deliberate thump.

I chuckled despite myself. "Great. Taking relationship advice from a dog. That's where I'm at."

At my admission, Chance stood and started to bark, sharp, urgent barks that cut through the quiet like a gunshot, shattering the fragile stillness of the forest. Every hair on the back of my neck stood on end. The dog was rigid, his muscles coiled tight as he stared down the path Sam had taken. His ears flicked forward, his tail low but twitching in agitation.

"What is it, boy?" I asked, tightening my grip on the crutch. I shifted my weight forward, testing my injured ankle, but Chance barked again—louder this time, insistent. His body quivered with tension, his gaze locked ahead.

Something was wrong.

A sharp pang of worry shot through me, my chest tightening. Sam could handle herself—hell, she was the strongest, most capable person I'd ever met—but even the best got caught off guard. And out here? The wild didn't care how tough you were.

"Sam!" I called, my voice rough, cutting through the damp air.

No answer.

The woods swallowed my shout, the whisper of wind in the trees mocking my unease. Chance let out another bark, his stance unwavering, his whole body screaming *move*.

I cursed under my breath, shifting unsteadily. I needed to act. Even if I was slower than I wanted, even if every step sent fire up my damn leg—I had to move.

All I could think about was Sam.

SAM

The path twisted sharply ahead, the mud thick and slick beneath my boots, threatening to steal my footing with every step. I moved carefully, picking my way forward, scanning the ground for stable footing for any hidden hazards that could send me sprawling. I'd been on worse trails, in worse conditions, but my mind wasn't on the terrain.

Chance wasn't at my side. I'd sent him back to stay with Ryan, knowing the dog would ensure he was okay. It was the right call, the logical choice. But his absence left a strange hollowness beside me.

I knew that hollow feeling wasn't just about Chance. It was about Ryan too—the way he'd looked at me, his eyes burning with something I wasn't ready to face. The way his words had cut through my carefully constructed walls like they were nothing more than paper.

"Things happen," he'd echoed, disbelief coloring his voice.

I'd been cruel. I knew it the moment the words left my mouth. But cruelty was easier than honesty—easier than admitting that what happened between us had shaken me in ways I couldn't afford.

The trail narrowed ahead, winding between two large boulders. Mud had collected in the space between them, creating a slick, treacherous patch that would be difficult to navigate. I slowed my pace, studying the best approach.

That's when I heard it—the sharp, urgent sound of barking.

My breath stalled. My head snapped up.

Chance.

My heart slammed against my ribs. The barking came again, louder, more insistent. A warning.

Something was wrong.

"Chance?" My voice cut through the trees, but the only response was another sharp, frantic bark.

Panic fired through my veins, and before I could think, I was sprinting back the way I'd come, mud splashing up my legs with every desperate step.

Please be okay. Please be okay.

I skirted past fallen branches, heart hammering against my ribs. My mind conjured a dozen scenarios—Ryan collapsed, his ankle worse than we thought, or maybe something else entirely. A wild animal. A rockslide.

The trail curved sharply, and suddenly there they were. Ryan was on his feet, leaning heavily on his makeshift crutch, his face tight with concern. Chance stood rigid beside him, ears forward, still barking urgently.

"Ryan!" I called, my voice sharp with urgency as I closed the distance between us. My boots skidded on the slick ground, but I didn't care—I needed to see him and make sure he was okay.

I stopped beside him, scanning him for injuries. "Are you hurt?" My breath came fast, adrenaline still surging through me.

His blue eyes locked onto mine, a flicker of relief flashing across his face before confusion set in. "Am I—what the hell, Sam?" he demanded, breathless. "Chance was going crazy—I thought something happened to *you*."

I turned to Chance, who now sat calmly next to Ryan, his tail wagging lazily, looking *far* too pleased with himself. My breath came in uneven bursts as it clicked. My chest deflated.

"You little—" I shook my head in disbelief, pressing a hand to my forehead. "He *tricked* us."

Ryan frowned. "What?"

"Chance tricked us into thinking something was wrong," I muttered, more to myself than him.

Ryan stared at Chance with dawning realization. "Wait, you mean he—"

"He faked an emergency," I confirmed, glaring at my dog who now sat with his tongue lolling out, looking satisfied.

"He faked an emergency to get us back together?" Ryan gestured between us, realization dawning.

"Apparently." I admitted, embarrassment heating my face.

Ryan's lips twitched. "Smart dog."

"Manipulative dog," I corrected, but there was no real heat behind my words. I reached out to scratch Chance behind the ears, unable to stay mad at him. "You're a menace, you know that?"

Ryan's laugh broke through the tension, a warm, rich sound that somehow made everything lighter. "So your dog's playing matchmaker now? That's a first."

Chance's tail thumped happily against the muddy ground, his amber eyes shifting between us with what could only be described as smug satisfaction.

"I can't believe I fell for that." He shook his head, running a hand through his damp hair. "Gave me a heart attack, but..." his voice trailed off, eyes meeting mine with that same intensity that had been there since last night. "Got you to come running back."

My heart skipped the admission hanging in the air between us. I couldn't look away from him, couldn't pretend I hadn't been terrified at the thought of him being hurt. The realization settled like a weight in my chest—I cared about him. More than I wanted to admit.

"You scare me, Anderson," I admitted, the words slipping out before I could stop them.

Ryan's smirk vanished. He stepped closer, his voice just as raw, just as honest.

"You scare me too."

Chapter Seven

♥

RYAN

For a moment, neither of us moved. The space between us buzzed with something heavy, unspoken—but undeniable.

Then Sam made the first move.

She dropped her pack and crashed into me, her lips urgent and unyielding, and every thought in my head disappeared. My crutch slipped from my grip, hitting the ground with a dull thud, but I barely registered it. My arms were already around her, pulling her closer, letting go wasn't an option.

Her fingers tangled in my hair, nails scraping lightly against my scalp, sending a shiver down my spine. My hands mapped the curve of her back, tracing the body I'd memorized in the firelight. She nipped at my bottom lip, and a deep groan rumbled from my chest before I could stop it.

Without breaking the kiss, I backed her up until she hit the rough bark of an oak tree. She gasped at the contact, but I swallowed the sound, pressing against her, surrounding her. Heat pulsed between us, and my hands tightened at her waist, holding her there like I could keep this moment from slipping away.

She wasn't just fire—she was wildfire, and I was done pretending I didn't want to burn.

With deft movements, I unfastened her belt and eased her pants down just enough. My fingers found her already slick and ready. She bit back a moan as I stroked her, her hips rocking against my hand.

"Turn around," I growled, my voice low and husky with desire.

Sam complied, bracing her hands against the tree trunk. The rough bark bit into her palms as I pressed close behind her. I reached down into her pack and grabbed a condom, slipping it on quickly. I entered her slowly, both of us groaning at the sensation. I set a steady rhythm, one hand gripping her hip while the other slid up beneath her shirt, my hand skimming over her breasts. I rolled her nipple between my fingers as I thrust deeper, drawing a low moan from her throat. She pressed back against me, meeting each thrust with equal fervor.

Our movements grew more frantic, more desperate. Sam's fingers dug into the bark of the tree, anchoring herself as pleasure built within her. She gasped as my hand slid lower, my fingers finding her sensitive bundle of nerves. I circled it in time with my thrusts.

"That's it, Sam," I murmured, feeling her inner walls flutter. "I want to hear how good I'm making you feel."

My words broke something loose inside her. She cried out, no longer able to hold back.

"Oh god Ryan," she gasped, her voice breathy and desperate. "Don't stop... please don't stop..."

I groaned at the sound of my name on her lips. I increased my pace, driving into her with deep, powerful thrusts. My fingers moved faster against her clit, pushing her closer to the edge.

"Come for me, Sam," I growled. "I want you to fucking come for me!"

And with one final thrust, we both reached our peak together, our bodies trembling with the intensity of our pleasure as we rode out the waves of ecstasy.

Sam's breath came in ragged gasps as she leaned against the tree, her body still trembling with aftershocks. My forehead rested against her shoulder, my arms wrapped tightly around her waist. For several long moments, the only sound was our labored breathing and the gentle rustle of leaves overhead.

Slowly, reality crept back in, cutting through the haze of heat and urgency. My breath was ragged, my pulse still hammering, but awareness settled over me like the cooling mountain air.

I loosened my grip, my hands resting on her waist, fingers flexing as if reluctant to let go.

She turned in my arms, her movements slower now, controlled. When her eyes met mine, a flicker of something unguarded passed between us, something raw and honest.

I didn't speak—I didn't need to. Instead, I leaned in, brushing my lips against hers, this time not out of desperation but something more deliberate.

SAM

I pushed away from the tree, my legs still shaky as I adjusted my clothing, my breath coming in uneven bursts. The bark had left rough imprints on my palms, tiny crescents where I'd gripped too hard, trying to anchor myself in a storm I hadn't seen coming.

Ryan watched me, his eyes tracking every movement as I steadied myself. He didn't reach for me again—giving me space, letting me gather myself—but I could feel the weight of his gaze, heavy with things neither of us had put into words.

Every nerve ending still hummed with aftershocks, my body remembering his touch even as I tried to collect myself. The forest around us seemed impossibly quiet now, as if holding its breath, waiting.

I finally broke the silence, my voice rough but steady. "So... what now?"

Ryan exhaled, his fingers brushing absently over his shirt's wrinkles. "That depends... are we walking away from this like nothing happened, or are we finally being honest about what's been building between us?"

He hesitated and then continued on. "I don't know what this is yet, Sam. But I know I'm not walking away from it."

I swallowed, my chest tightening at the quiet conviction in his voice. "Even if I don't make it easy?"

Ryan huffed out a laugh, shaking his head. "You? Difficult? Never."

I rolled my eyes, but the warmth curling in my stomach wouldn't be ignored. "You sure you're up for this, Anderson? I don't do halfway. If we do this, I need to know you're all in."

Ryan pushed off the tree, wincing slightly as he adjusted his stance. His hand found mine, rough and warm, his fingers threading through mine like it was the most natural thing in the world. "I don't do halfway either," he said, his voice low, steady. "So yeah, Sam. I'm all in."

I squeezed his hand, fighting the smile that threatened to break free. "Alright then," I murmured. "Guess we'd better get off this mountain."

Ryan grinned, giving my fingers a light tug. "Lead the way, Monroe. Just try not to leave me in the dust."

I smirked, squeezing his hand one last time before letting go. "No promises."

Epilogue

♥

SAM

The late afternoon sun bathed Anchor Bay in a soft, golden glow as Ryan pulled his truck into the parking lot of Milo's veterinary clinic. I glanced into the back-seat, where Chance sat, tail thumping against the leather, his entire body vibrating with excitement.

"Someone's excited," Ryan said, smirking as he caught Chance's eager expression in the rearview mirror.

I chuckled, shaking my head. "A post-mission spa day is probably his favorite thing."

Ryan parked and shut off the engine. "Can't blame him. If Milo had a human day spa, I'd sign up, too."

Rolling my eyes, I stepped out just as Chance barked and pawed at the window, more than ready to get going.

I opened the back door, and he leaped out, circling me in happy loops before sitting at my side like the perfect gentleman.

The familiar scent of cedarwood and something faintly herbal drifted from the clinic as we approached. Inside, Milo stood behind the counter, a lazy, easygoing grin spreading across his face.

"Morning," he greeted, crouching down to give Chance a well-earned scratch behind the ears. "Ready for your day of luxury, big guy?"

Chance let out a soft woof, his tail wagging so hard his entire body swayed.

"We'll be back in a couple of hours," I said, passing Milo the leash. "Let me know if he gives you any trouble."

Milo scoffed. "Trouble? This guy? He's an angel compared to some of my other customers."

Just then the door swung open behind us and a woman rushed in, cradling a small bundle of fur.

"Milo!" she called, dark hair slipping free from a messy bun as she hurried toward him. "I need your help—this little guy's in bad shape."

Milo let out a sharp breath, already bracing himself. "Penelope," he said, his tone edged with exasperation. "What have you dragged in this time?"

"A fox," she said breathlessly, ignoring his tone. "Found him near the bakery this morning. He was limping—I think his paw's broken."

Ryan and I exchanged glances as Penelope barreled forward, her concerned gaze locked on the injured animal.

Milo muttered something but didn't hesitate, already moving toward an exam table. "Bring him here," he instructed his tone all business now.

Penelope followed, carefully settling the fox down. Her fingers skimmed lightly over its fur, her expression tight with worry. "I didn't know where else to take him."

Milo sighed, scrubbing a hand down his face. "Of course you didn't." But when he glanced at the fox, something in his demeanor shifted. His hands were gentle as he checked the animal, his focus narrowing. "You should've called first."

"And risk you saying no?" Penelope shot back, one eyebrow lifting.

Milo's jaw ticked, but he didn't argue. Instead, he exhaled slowly, his voice gruff but quieter now. "You can't save everything, Pen."

Her expression softened just a fraction. "Doesn't mean I won't try."

Milo shook his head, but his hands were steady as he continued his exam. "Yeah," he muttered. "I've noticed."

I nudged Ryan, my voice low with amusement. "What do you think?"

His grin was slow, knowing. "Can't wait to see how this plays out."

As we left the clinic, leaving Chance in Milo's capable hands, Ryan draped an arm over my shoulders. The warmth of his touch, his solid presence beside me—it f elt... right. The kind of right I hadn't let myself believe in for a long time.

For once, I didn't second-guess it.

***

Dear Reader,

Thank you so much for reading *Falling for the Rescue*! I hope you loved Ryan and Sam's story—their fiery tension, undeniable chemistry, and the battle between their hardened independence and the pull of something deeper. Writing their journey was an adventure, and I'm so grateful you came along for the ride.

If you enjoyed the book, I'd truly appreciate it if you took a moment to leave a review. Reviews help authors like me connect with more readers, and even a few words can make a huge difference in sharing these stories. You can review *Falling for the Rescue* **here: https://www.amazon.com/dp/B0DZ1D2S8G**

Thank you for your support—I can't wait to bring you more heart-pounding, high-heat romances filled with sparks, adventure, and unforgettable connections!

With gratitude,

Hana York

***

Loved *Falling for the Rescue*? Don't miss the rest of the *Hearts on Duty* series! Each book is packed with swoon-worthy heroes, strong heroines, and plenty of sparks. If you haven't read them yet, here's what you're missing:

Book One

Sparks of Temptation

A sizzling small-town romance where forced proximity turns up the heat between a stubborn chef and a protective firefighter. Olivia Harper came to Anchor Bay for a fresh start—not a flirty distraction. After rebuilding her life, she has no time for complications, especially the kind that come with broad shoulders, a cocky grin, and a hero complex. Jack Lawson knows how to keep his cool under pressure. As a firefighter, protecting people is second nature. But

Olivia? She doesn't want rescuing, and she sure as hell doesn't want him getting too close. When a plumbing mishap lands him as her unexpected housemate, their battle of wills turns into something neither of them can ignore. The problem? Olivia has spent years proving she doesn't need anyone, while Jack's instincts tell him to stand back before he wants something he can't have. But some flames refuse to die out... Get *Sparks of Temptation* on Amazon today: https://www.amazon.com/dp/B0DXJFFS11

Book Two

Love's Anchor

A sizzling small-town romance where years of friendship ignite into something neither of them can ignore. Brooke Taylor has spent years keeping her feelings for Theo Morgan buried beneath sharp comebacks and stubborn denial. As a no-nonsense cop in Anchor Bay, she's never let emotions get in the way of the job—especially when it comes to the charming, frustrating bar owner who knows exactly how to push her buttons. Theo has always played it safe when it comes to Brooke. She's his best friend, his steady constant—the one woman he can't afford to lose. But when a break-in at his bar forces them into close quarters, the tension between them finally boils over. Can they risk their friendship to take a chance on love? Or will fear keep them apart forever? Get *Love's Anchor* on Amazon today: https://www.amazon.com/dp/B0DY66VX6Q

Book Three

On Call for You

He swore she was off-limits. She's ready to prove him wrong. Dr. Sophie Whitaker has spent her career proving herself in a world that underestimates her. As a brilliant but petite doctor, she's fought for respect every step of the way. Moving back to Anchor Bay is supposed to be a fresh start—not a temptation in the form of Lucas Carter. The rugged EMT with a cocky grin and a hero complex. The man her brother trusts with his life... and the one she should definitely stay away from. Lucas Carter lives by two rules: stay cool under pressure and never, ever cross the line with Sophie Whitaker. Even if she's gorgeous. Even if she's sharp-witted and impossible to ignore. Even if, after one stormy encounter stranded together, the idea of walking away feels damn near impossible. Now, every stolen glance and lingering touch has Lucas questioning everything—especially the rule that's kept him from going after the one woman he can't stop thinking about. Falling for Sophie could mean risking his oldest friendship. But walking away? That might be the biggest mistake of his life. Get *On Call for You* on Amazon

today: https://www.amazon.com/dp/B0D
Y6RKD5Y

Book Four

Investigating Desire

**A Slow-Burn Romantic Suspense with
a Grumpy Detective and the Journalist
Who Won't Back Down**

Detective Nate Whitaker has sworn off love.
After a messy divorce, he's buried himself
in his work, content to keep his emotions
locked away. But when a bold, relentless
journalist starts shadowing him for an exclusive story, their push-and-pull dynamic ig-
nites a slow burn neither of them can ignore.
Tessa Donovan has worked hard to make a
name for herself. She's determined to crack
open a case that's rocked this small town,

even if it means getting under the skin of a brooding detective who wants nothing to do with her. But when her investigation stirs up danger, Nate has no choice but to keep her close. What starts as a reluctant partnership turns into something far more dangerous—a fiery attraction neither of them is ready for. With a growing threat looming and tension crackling between them, this small-town romantic suspense is about to heat up. Can Nate and Tessa untangle the case before it's too late, or will their undeniable chemistry turn into the biggest risk of all? Get *Investigating Desire* on Amazon today: https://www.amazon.com/dp/B0DYZYCS1D

Hana York Books

♥

Hearts on Duty Series

Sparks of Temptation

Love's Anchor

On Call for You

Investigating Desire

Falling for the Rescue

For a full list of titles, please visit Hana York's website

www.HanaYork.com

About the Author

♥

Hana York writes fast-paced, heart-pounding contemporary romance packed with irresistible heroes, strong heroines, laugh-out-loud banter, and just the right amount of spice to keep things sizzling. Her books are for readers who love grumpy men falling hard, fierce women who don't need saving, and the kind of chemistry that sparks off the page.

When she's not crafting stories full of love, tension, and toe-curling moments, you'll find her daydreaming about small-town charm, plotting ridiculous meet-cutes, and consuming an unhealthy amount of coffee. She believes in happily-ever-afters, overprotective heroes who don't stand a chance against their heroines, and that every great love story should come with a side of sass.

If you love forced proximity, off-limits attraction, sizzling tension, and romance that makes your heart race, welcome to the world of Hana York!

Follow Hana York for new releases, exclusive content, and behind-the-scenes fun! Visit www.HanaYork.com for more information.

Find all her books here: https://www.amazon.com/author/hanayork

Follow her on Instagram here: https://www.instagram.com/hanayorkromance/

Follow her on Facebook here: https://www.facebook.com/profile.php?id=61572569228900

Follow her on Goodreads here: https://www.goodreads.com/author/show/54826946.Hana_York

Join her mailing list here: https://www.hanayork.com/subscribe